T0062819

MY TWO YEARS CRUSH

MY TWO YEARS CRUSH

Or Maybe Love???

PRANOTI JARIWALA

PARTRIDGE
A Penguin Random House Company

To order additional copies of this book, contact
Partridge India
000 800 10062 62
orders.india@partridgepublishing.com

www.partridgepublishing.com/india

TO EVERYONE WHO READS THIS BOOK

"FOREVER IS A LIE- EVEN ROMEO HAS TO DIE."

AUTHOR'S NOTE

THANK YOU READERS FOR PICKING UP MY BOOK. Whatever I'll get, thanks to all my readers.

Before starting to say anything about my book, I first of all wish to remember about the people who have helped me to become the person who I'm. We all have different stories-some different, beautiful and lovely love stories. Let me remind you all about the Disney world. Cinderella walked on the broken glass while Sleeping beauty had let a whole lifetime pass. Belle fell in love with a hideous beast while Jasmine married a common thief. Ariel walked on land for love and Snow White barely escaped a knife. It was all about blood, sweat and tears. Because Love means facing your biggest fears.

I, first of all want to thank someone there in the big white clouds up there. Almighty. I know you have always been as a shadow to me.

But sorry before you I have somebody else. And they are my parents. Thank you MOM and DADDY without you I am nothing. MOM-You have always been my best friend and DADDY-My first love. You are the one I know who will never disappoint me.

My Sister PARSHADI and my brother VRAJESH and my siblings DRASHTI, TRUSHTI, HAIMIN and MAHEK-You all are a very important part of my life. I thank you for supporting me to overcome my every obstacle.

Then How can I forget those school days? Memories which are still fresh in my mind. TANYA, ADITI, DHRUVA, JESSICA, ANISHA, ALVINA and RENUKA school days can never be perfect without you all. Bitter and sweet memories makes me still nostalgic. TANVI, MUGDHA, MANSI and MARIYA-You have been all the time I wanted. Thank you for being the best persons of my life.

I sincerely want to thank MISS.NAMRATA TALEGAONKAR, Thank you ma'am you have been the first person who comes to my mind when I remember about my novel. Thank you for telling me all the beautiful compliments and encouraging me about my novel.

I also want to thank my friend NAVIN BHANUSHALI-without whom I would have not taken the first step of getting my novel published. Thank you friend for all your support.

I thank my college friends RUTVA, ANKUR, YUVRAJ, SHIVANSHU, UTSAV, NEEL, KISHAN, HARDIK, DIVYA, RITU, DARSHAN, VICKY, DHAVAL, SAMARTH-Thank you all of you from my inner heart as you all have explained me what beauty life has.

KRISH, JATIN, ABHI AND PRAHARSH-You are the gems of my life. Thank you for having me in your life. I thank that almighty to bless me with such lovely people in my life.

Hostel life is so incomplete without the people I met there. BHUMI, DEVANGI, PALAK, KRUSHITA, HIRAL, DHARA, HEENA, NEETU, FATEMA, HEMALI-Thank you all for letting me know all the good and bad aspects of my life.

I want to thank my friend DEVANG SAROLIYA for this beautiful cover.

The entire team of penguin partridge publishing, India.

I want to thank every person who has helped me in this new and beautiful journey. To get my first novel published.

I THANK ALL THE PEOPLE I KNOW WHO HAVE BEEN MY GREATEST SUPPORT, MY STRENGTH, MY FEAR AND MY BEST FRIENDS.

I want my novel to reach to as many people I can-I am human so maybe I have some corrections and ups and downs. If possible, I'd like my readers to support me and mould me to become a good author.

Give me your love and support. Your love can win through all my goals.

Common people join me in reading this beautiful story where you may find love, friends, memories, breakups, patchups, mischief's because that is all life is about……………..

PROLOGUE

Do you think one-sided love stories ever exist? Do you think true love can be one-sided? And maybe it's not true, but someone can love someone truly but fate doesn't meet up at the end.

What is that feeling called if not one-sided true love? Or maybe you feel it is the love of your life, but you have to let him go....

But she more than loves him and cannot cease to love him, maybe. Think of her, sometimes when the Alps and oceans would divide them-but they never will unless his wish.

And his wish is temporary as he is unaware of her undying love for him or maybe she would be happy without him in his life. Here's the story of a happy yet scared yet funny MAYRA who falls for REHAN and their tale-a one-sided love story

"Take this kiss upon the brow!

And, in parting from you now...

Thus much let me avow-

You are not wrong, whom deem,

That my days have been a dream,

Yet if hope has flown away,

In a night, or in a day,

In a vision, or in none,

Is it therefore the less gone??

All that we see or seem,

Is but a dream within a dream!

I stand amid the roar, Of a surf-tormented shore,

And I hold within my hand, Grains of the golden sand.

How few! Yet how they creep, Though my fingers to the deep,

While I weep, while I weep!

O God! Can I not grasp, Them with a tighter clasp?

Out from the pitiless wave?

O God! Can I not save, Is all that we see or seem,

But a beautiful dream within a dream...!

ONE

The curtains had been wide open for quite some time now letting the yellow rays of the sun stream through the open window onto the face of the sleepy MAYRA, who lay in her bed covered with the silk yellow colored cloth with little knots on the side, which I usually used to play with during night.

Very comfortable in my sleep but still unmoving. My eyes flickered through the dawn and my fingers trembled. I was asleep and did not want to wake up. It was a good-night's sleep.

Finally, after tossing from side-to-side, I was woken up by my aunt who was in a hurry to inform me about my 10th board results being declared that very same morning.

My eyes refused to wake up but I had to because I had to check my results. It was 6a.m. and I moved out of the cozy bed and walked out of my room in the purple night dress, barefooted and all hair messy covering my eyes which were half-asleep. Rubbing my eyes, I walked and sat in front of my PC screen and typed "www.gseb.org" in the Google search. Eager to know my result I typed my "seat no.B-700320" and my result is displayed.

15

Overall grade *B2* and percentile rank *92.93* displayed in bold letters on the computer screen. I was rejoiced by seeing my result and called up my mom. The phone rang twice when finally my mom answered.

"Good Morning, beta"

I happily wished her good morning and said,

"Guess what? My results are out and I scored 92.93 in my 10th boards."

My mom congratulated me and was also eager to know the marks of my twin NATASHA who still was in her dreams very fast asleep.

"She scored a 65, Mom" I said with an encouraging voice.

"Good! The two of you scored well" My mom replied.

I hugged my aunt in a jolly mood and went back to bed with my teddy bear who was the best thing I ever had in my life.

Things were changing. I knew I was growing up and it was the time when I have to decide my career goals.

"Science stream", I shouted to my Mom, when she asked me what I wanted to study further.

My sister wanted to opt for architecture but had skipped the "NATA" exams so she too opted for science stream along with me. It was the same school I got admitted to where I was studying since the last 12 Years.

"LOURDES CONVENT HIGH SCHOOL", a typical girls school where girls wore a short blue-checks skirt along with white plain shirt tucked in with a blue checks tie round the neck, two plaited hairs and the same black 'adidas' shoes. But the best part was cottie we got to wear only for the higher secondary students symbolizing our superiority.

A different yet funny, amazing life was about to begin where I had my own dreams and wishes to fulfill and live a happening life ahead. Vacations ended and now it was time for my 11th Semester-1 to start.

TWO

First day. A new semester has started and I was all set to enjoy my year ahead. As usual the day started with the morning assembly at school with the singing of the Christian carols and some speech of the day including the thought of the day and the national anthem at the end. New friends, New class 11-D which read "SCIENCE STREAM", new teachers everything new.

I walked up to the classroom with my new bag in a good neat uniform and two plaited hair. Most of my classmates knew me as I studied in this school since last 12 years.

There were many new students who took admission and joined 11-D this year. It was very amazing to have only one science class 11-D, the rest 11-A, 11-B and 11-C where commerce classes.

I choose to sit on the bench near the back-door where my friends usually sat. The first day started with introduction with our new teachers including our class teacher Mrs.Smita. She was a very calm and peaceful lady who had a boy cut haircut and wore silk sari. She was our class teacher, beautiful yet a little strict.

I knew her before as she was known to me during my 10th classes. She was my Social Science teacher.

Next was my physics teacher Ms.Sweta. She was very thin and tall-heighted. A very calm bachelor and a good physics teacher as well. I loved to talk to her as she was very good at explaining things to me easily even during my Practical labs.

Then came our chemistry sir Mr. Mathew. He had an south-Indian accent of speaking though he was not. He was a very hardworking person but I often misunderstood what he taught us during the lectures as due to his speech. We usually used to make fun of him due to his speech.

Apart from them I had Ms.Indu as my mathematics teacher. A south-Indian lady with the great knowledge about Maths. I always wonder to have her mind during my maths exams as she could solve each sum so quickly. Ms.Indu use to apply a lot of make-up on her face.

My computer madam Ms.Mona and biology teacher Mrs.Farnaz were also the great in their own fields.

Friends are the major part in one's life. So were my friends.

"The most amazing group or we can say the funniest group of 11-D".

I was not ready for all this as life seemed to be easy for me until I had to attend my tuitions also along with my school.

My mom had found a good tuition for me and Natasha as we also needed some extra practices to study. I went to the tuition where one of my elder sisters joined earlier when they were in their secondary classes. Now they studied pharmacy at college. I was scared because I never went to a cuot tuition before.

Until now my life was captured in the girl's school and the private tuitions where I didn't have to face much public. But now it's a different scenario.

I walked up to the new "CITYLIGHT COMPLEX" where my rickshaw-wala dropped me and my sister.

"Come at 8:00 to pick us back", I said to him and he drove back.

First I had to attend my maths tuition which was away from the complex. Mr.Ashok Lad was my mathematics sir who was very talented and use to teach maths since last few years.

I stepped inside the class and sat there along with Natasha by my side. On my other side there was a girl who wore a black t-shirt along with some her dark blue jeans and a book and a pen in her hand. I looked at her, she looked at me. We smiled at each other.

Soon the class got full and there were a few of some 30 students. There were all new faces in front of me. But I knew I would be good to everyone.

Our classes got completed early as it was the first day. I, Natasha and two of her new bachmates sat outside on the swing waiting for my richkshaw-wala to arrive.

"What's your name?" I asked the girl besides me in a pale voice.

"Mugdha", she replied.

"Dhvani", the other girl replied too.

We were good at each other and become good friends in a short period of time. Our next class was the physics class. Again the same rush, new people around me, new place but I still somehow managed to enter the class. I and Natasha sat along the side where the other girls sat and our class started which was conducted by Mr.Murtuza and it went well again.

Followed by it was my chemistry class conducted by Mr.Bhati. It was the noisiest class I ever had attended. I entered the class and went and sat on the second bench. I got an awkward feeling as the girls there were a bit of attitude class.

"Not talking to a new girl besides you is what sort of attitude", I whispered to my own self.

Just at that moment a girl sitting beside me who worn a pink checks t-shirt, white jeans, very fair and one plaited hair on the left side of her shoulder looked at me and said.

"Tum kuch bolte nahi ho kya?"

I looked at her in a little amazement and said.

"No. It's not like that. I'm just a little scared of such noisy place."

She stretched her hand towards me and said, "Hey! I'm Aaliya". I smiled at her and replied, "Hey, I'm Mayra".

She started talking to a girl sitting in front of us on the first bench and introduced me to her. She was Dharti Patel, who studied at the biology class along with Aal. Soon we became good friends as we had the same school and tuitions and we usually spent the most of our time together.

On the third day of our tuition class, I still had an awkward feeling as other people were still not making much contact with me. I was very touched by that and thought this is not the correct place for me.

I walked up to my mom later that evening and cried in front of her.

"What happen, dear? Why are you crying answer me?" my mom asked me in a silent voice.

"This all is not meant for me, Mumma. I'm scared to talk to new people and I don't like to visit such places", I replied to her again bursting into tears.

She calmly kissed my forehead and replied, "Mayra, this is a new world for you now. Let some days pass by, and you'll start enjoying this world. Maybe you're scared now but this life will lead you to a successful way ahead. Don't cry my girl; Mumma knows Mayra is a strong girl"

I looked at her and gave a slight smile. She kissed my forehead again and I went to sleep keeping her words in mind.

THREE

School days are the best days anyone can have in their life. Such were the days with me also. As mumma said I started liking this new world a few days later when I had interactions with my fellow class mates and my joyful friends.

Our school group was one of the famous groups in our class. These people made school days worth-living. As introduced earlier Aaliya and Dharti were two of the members of our group along with me and Natasha.

One was Tanie Koreth, a rich Christian girl with adventuring nature. She loved to visit places and was even very fluent in her English skills. She hated study a little more but was a very cool friend of mine.

Annie Fernandas, a simple Christian girl who was very familiar to me. The greatest similarity between Me and her was that we had a big-fat crush on the same person and who was no other than "SURESH-RAINA". Every single match of Raina would make me and Annie shout like mad at each other. We would talk rubbish about going and meeting Raina and all girly desires.

Next was Jess Cesar, a short heighted dark complexion girl who was also a part of our group.

I and jess did not talk much as I did not like to talk to her due to her behavior. Though we were good friends but still there was a little cat-fight between us.

Other was Aditi Patel, a perfect gujju girl who with her sweet Gujarati accent used to talk a lot. Blah-blah-blah was her favorite hobby. She was a good friend of mine.

Renu Miglani, was the BHAI of our group. A typical Haryanvi girl who was very good at making people laugh with her silly jokes. She was also one of the girl who wore the "KADA" along with me.

Next was Dharti Patel, a sweet yet soft hearted girl who was "BEST-FRIEND" of mine. She was short heighted, fair complexion and an intelligent girl who would with her sweet talks can please anybody. With a short period of time I and Dharti became best friends and we used to talk for hours not even a single minute left without talking. She was a special friend of mine. Say my bench-mate, my crime-partner or my anything else.

These people made school days much better. It was the time for our biology and mathematics class when Annie, Jess, Natasha, Adi, Renu and me where in the Maths class while Dharti, Aal and Tannie went for their biology class upstairs.

"Limits and derivatives", shouted our maths teacher in a loud voice.

I was shocked to hear as she had conducted a surprise test for the mathematics students.

"I don't know any of the answers, Adi", I said to Adi.

"So do I", replied she.

At that moment Aal, Dharti and Tannie came to the class to collect their class calendar from their respective bags.

"What happened guys? What's the matter?" asked Natasha to Tannie.

"Nothing we are being taken to the principal's office!" she said in a high voice.

We looked at each other in amazement and started laughing with a loud voice. It was seriously funny but my friends were taken to the principal's office because they rang the school bell during the going lectures. Teachers were shocked to hear the school bell ring between the period and the victim was caught due to the cameras on each floor's.

Aal, Dharti and Tannie stood outside the principal's office when their parents arrived at the school reception.

"Why did you ring the bell?" asked our principal in a harsh voice to the three of them.

"Just to see whether it really rang or was kept just like that!" replied Aal in a low voice.

The principal was shocked to hear such an answer and they were punished for such pranks due to the stake of school reputation.

Days became a merry along with them. Each day a new prank, few bunks, few gossips and eating Tiffin boxes during the recess time added beauty to each and every day that grew by. The teachers would scold us for our new pranks but still encouraged us to be good students and work harder for the semester results.

Tuition days were a jolly. Meeting one and the same people everyday yet so enjoyable. New friends and new ideas. The lectures were boring yet very interesting to watch the boys sitting on the opposite benches and giggling and laughing would continue.

FOUR

Our physics tuition was about to start and all of the students were ready sitting on their benches. Girls sat in the girls section while the boys sat in the boys section. It was 4 p.m. in the clock when my sir arrived in the classroom to make us study the topic further.

I was playing with my pen and listening to Dharti about the projects we were assigned for the school semester that time. At that moment the door opened and someone walked in and went ahead to look for a place to sit. Sir called him and suggested him to sit on the second bench.

I was watching that guy with a mere look and didn't know why I was doing that. Our tuition had attendance system in which attendance was usually given through the electronic system in our class. Just put your thumb near the machine and the light glows. If it's a red light you're absent and if it's a green then you're present.

At the end of the class, Sir asked that boy to submit the assignment question papers all over the class. I was not able to understand for a second what was happening all around but was a little tensed when he was coming closer and closer to my bench. He wore a black colored shirt and blue light color jeans. He wore simple Slippers which suited his legs properly. His eyes were covered with his long small crissed-crossed hair and his eyes were covered with his black framed specs with red frame beside.

He came near my bench and started giving the papers one-by-one. I looked down and did not make any eye contact with him. He gave me the papers one after the other and I kept on passing the other side. At last he gave mine. I looked at him; there was a slight smile onto his face which took my heart.

He distributed the papers all over the class and went and sat again in his respective place. The attendance sheet came at the end of the class where sir announced the name of the students who missed out to give their attendance. As usual I was listening to the names when,

"Rehan", announced sir in his mike.

The boy whom I noticed raised his hand and the sir marked him present. I got a chill in my stomach when I got to hear his name. Soon the class ended and we went to the chemistry class. He accompanied me there too and I was glad about that.

"Look, Dharti the guy next to the blue t-shirt one", I said to Dharti pointing towards Rehan.

"Looks handsome", replied Dharti in a naughty manner.

I was eager to learn more about Rehan. Every day I waited for him to arrive at the tuitions at 4 p.m. I was eager to know his surname, his family his school everything. I called up Dharti and Aal and went upstairs to the maths class where results were displayed for the first test conducted last week.

"Rehan Soni, Rehan Patel??" I read from the list and looked at Dharti.

"So there are two of the boys named Rehan", Dharti answered my question.

We left the place then as it was 8:00 and we had to leave for home now. I went home and completed my dinner and went quickly and sat in front of the computer screen.

Though I did not have a face book account I logged in from my mom's account and types "Rehan Soni" in the search box.

A picture of a boy was on the sea shore as the display picture. I was not able to recognize Rehan and switched to type "Rehan Patel" in the search box. Though my effort that night I still was not able to recognize Rehan's surname and I logged off from my Mom's id. I went to bed and slept. Few days the same thing happened when I would wait for him and used to look at him on the time when he's not looking at me.

After the maths classes me and Mugdha was standing near the parked vehicles in the complex. I saw Rehan coming from upstairs. I had mentioned Mugdha about Rehan during one of my talks to her.

"Mugdha, See this is the guy whom I talked about to you", I said to her in a rejoicing voice.

"This guy? Seriously?" she asked me in an amazed voice.

"Yes", I answered along with a questioning face.

"This guy is in my class at school. He sits behind my bench and his name is Rehan Soni and he is a good friend of mine", replied Mugdha with a swift voice.

I just looked at her and gave her a huge smile and hugged her and thanked her so much to let me know his name. I was very happy that day.

Soon I came to know about him. I started liking his looks, his naughty behavior yet cute smile, his way of walking and the different clothes he wore which perfectly suited his body. The most important was his 'WILSON' titled bag which always gave me a hint that it was Rehan.

Rehan also started to have weird yet cute looks at me. I started noticing the place he used to sit in every class and also he would notice the place I sit during every lecture.

Days passed and there by the eagerness of talking to him was getting more and more. But I felt shy talking to him. And so did him.

It was 25th of August and it was Dharti's birthday. We all had planned a good surprise for her. She was looking beautiful in her purple dress and purple framed specs.

"Happy Birthday, Dharu", I wished her at midnight without forgetting to wake up. Thanks to my alarm.

"Thank you sooo much dear", replied Dharti in a happy voice.

The day well went as we celebrated her birthday in a simple manner by wishing her best. The chocolate birthday cake was like a cherry on the cake for the day. She too was very happy as it was a simple birthday celebration yet a joyous one.

It was our physics class and we were on the topic of "Friction caused in the wheels of vehicles".

I was sitting at the left-most corner of the bench as I usually sit. Rehan came late that day so he had to sit on the bench just behind me. He sat exactly behind me.

"The wheels of the vehicle move with an indecisive force usually when they move on rough surfaces. At that time friction is produced in the wheels when they oppose the gravity. Usually when a vehicle is travelling on a slope e.g. a mountain"

Sir was explaining us about the topic when….

"CEAT-TYRES"

Someone said with a soft voice. It was the cutest-male voice I ever heard. It was Rehan's voice. It was the first time I heard his voice and I did not knew he had a cute voice along with that cute face which always had a slight smile on his face.

FIVE

"Which school is on your list for your first semester exams?" asked my mom.

"It's my own school, Mumma", I replied.

I was happy as my number was in my own school. Teachers knew me well so I was quite excited about it. Mugdha, Me and Dhvani had the same school as we had initials matching. It was a procedure where we had to go to the school assigned to us on the hall ticket and our exams are conducted there.

"It's English Exam today. Wish you luck. All the best", said by Grandmother to me.

I bowed towards her and replied "Thank you Nani"

I went to the temple at my place and bowed in front of god for my first paper and even wished for my paper to go well. Unfortunately this time I and Natasha had different schools as the examination centre so our parents decided to come along both of us individually. I went with my dad and Natasha was accompanied by my mom.

I was standing outside the school gate with my entire stuff-compass box, Clip-board and my hall ticket talking with Mugdha and her mom.

"Look Mayra someone's here!" said Mugdha in a rejoicing mood.

I looked at the opposite side of the road where there stood a boy in a pale light yellow colored t-shirt with his dad on one side and mom on the other. He was *"REHAN"*. I was so excited to see him.

"Oh my god! I and Rehan have the same examination center."

I was pretty well excited about the rest of the five examinations as Rehan was going to accompany me in them. Butterflies were flying in my mind and my heart always skipped a beat at the time I would see him. Exam was over and it went very well.

This continued until the next 5 days until the exams got over and now it was time for a vacation. I was not very much excited about the vacation as it would keep me away from Rehan. I would not be able to see him till many days.

"Ambaji and Mount Abu", said my Mom to me. When I asked her where were we going to visit during the vacation?

"Pack your bags and take up whatever you need. We will be leaving Surat the day after tomorrow", said my mom looking at me and Natasha.

I got very much excited as I always get because I love travelling especially with my family. I still remember the trip we had to south India when we visited KanniyaKumari, Rameshwaram, Ooty, Chennai and Hospet. The night at Hospet was a memory. Rainy Day, Dinner and all walking on the road all alone with just you sister besides you added beauty to the day. The heavy pores of the rain were the best experience I ever had.

Coming to the present we started our journey in our FIAT-PALIO. At the dawn of the day we started our journey to the pilgrimage place. Me and Ronak, my younger brother was the entire first from our place to get ready and sit with our respective luggages.

"Goggles-Done, Phone Charger-Done, Novels-Done, Snacks-Done, 5pair of clothes-checked.", Me and Ronak had a small checking before we were about to leave.

"All the three of you sleep as you woke up too early this morning", my mom said pointing towards dad to lock the house doors.

Finally we started off. I plugged my earphones in and was calm sitting towards the right-side of the back seat behind my father. Natasha sat towards the left behind my mother and Ronak sat in between us. Soon he was half asleep laying his head on one of my shoulders. Mom started to hear her morning prayers and dad busy driving as soon as possible. He says early morning drives are the fresh ones.

We did not forget to pay a visit at my grandfather's place as we usually do every time. We started our journey from Surat at 4 a.m. early morning.

Soon we crossed the national highway and at the dusk we were in the city of blessings, a city where people come to pray, to bow before the goddess of wealth, health and power-MAA Ambe.

We halted at our usual place-*Amdavad Ni dharamshala* which was in the middle of the city streets and nearer to the temple gates. It was a one or a half kilometer walking distance from there to the temple with the streets in-between.

We decided to visit the temple early next morning as it was a long day journey and my dad was quite tired due to constant driving.

"Sleep earlier today as we have to go to the temple tomorrow by 7 a.m.", my mom instructed my brother.

It was a good sleep in the Air conditioned room with two beds and two fans including two tube lights. A television for entertainment and a simple bath-room for the bathing and loo.

The outskirts were much better as it was a good verandah to sit in the evenings and a garden to play in. My brother and I usually played badminton there during our every visit. It was a routine to visit the place as my mom liked it very much.

Soon we got ready the next morning and were at the temple. The five of us walked in from the Gate no.3 which was behind the main temple. My dad and Ronak walked in to the MALE section and I, Mom and Natasha walked in to the FEMALE section.

We offered garlands and *chunari* to the goddess where it was a peaceful scenario in front of the heavenly goddess to bow and adore her some respect.

We soon left for the *Gabbar temple*, a place which stood on the hill. People can travel their through rope-ways or by climbing the 999 stairs to go up to the mountain which lead to the temple.

They say there is a *"deep jyot"* there which never extinguishes as it has presence of goddess there. We had our lunch at the restaurant there after we completed our prayers. In the evening, we roamed about the streets and did some shopping. My mom shopped some clothes for "Lord Krishna's idol" at our place and some jewellery. The day ended and we were back at our room. My father dimmed the light and we all went into deep slumber.

"Wake up and take your bath", shouted my mom at me.

I looked into my phone and it was just 5 a.m. I thought to myself why my mother in such a hurry was but then,

"OH! Shit- It's Mount Abu today!" I smirked at myself.

We all got ready up to 6 a.m. My dad was the last and the late-comer to get ready. We packed our bags and took it to the car.

My dad logged the luggage inside the car. He checked out and we were off to Rajasthan. We had our morning breakfast at the hotel near the hill-foot which had a combo of the Rajasthan and Guajarati food.

"90% Rajasthan is covered by the Gujarati's", said the waiter to my Dad while taking our order.

We had 5 cups of tea and 2 plates of batata-phoa and 1 plate of my favorite yellow fafda. Our tummy was full and we headed off to climb the mountain early morning.

It was a nice, cool humid weather with lovely birds chirping all around. The sun did not still rise. He hid behind the mountain ranges which were on the opposite sides. Natasha slept as she had a vomiting feeling when she usually travelled the mountains. Mom and Dad were busy in their talks and Ronak busy with his cam-coder. The music was ON in the car and everybody busy in their own world.

"Dil kyun yeh mera, shor kare, Dil kyun yeh mera shor kare,

Idhar nahi udhar nahi, Teri ore chale........"

Played the music system in our car. I was simply seeing outside the window shields, engaged deeply in a deep thought. I was thinking of Rehan. "What would he be doing?", "Where would he be?", "Would he be in Surat or somewhere else?"

Thoughts rolled down my mind with different innumerable funny questions which were un-answerable. Sometimes I think the songs and the lyrics where written seeing my situation. Whether I'm sad or happy, Music is the medium I have peace of mind. It is like a drug to my soul. It freshens up my mind and simply reminds me of someone I miss. Soon we reached Mount Abu.

We halted to the place my mother already booked last night. Late in the evening we visited the Nakki Lake. I, Natasha and Ronak were all set to click pictures and post it on face book. In this busy world no one is least busy to upload a picture to his face book wall. The current status, the current place and the current upload matters a lot rather than enjoying at that very moment.

We headed off to the sunset point late in that evening. One has to walk a long distance parking cars at the parking areas. Just climb the mountain stairs. Sit and wait for the red dark yellowed sun to set. And we were waiting for that moment. After a short period of time there he was, a yellow ball in the sky perfectly visible slowly and gradually hiding behind the mountains and waving a goodnight.

It was the most beautiful sunset I ever saw. We went back to our rooms as it was growing dark and slept early that night as we had to head off to my hometown the next day.

The week vacation was over and I was back to my studies.

I was happy this time as I was to see Rehan again after a long time. My friends were waiting for us to meet again after a little Span of time. Re-union's are a great pleasure no matter they are after a week or after some years.

Meeting old friends and recalling the silly things we used to do is one of the favorite parts I always loved to do. The second favorite thing was to make names for our crushes and enjoy to-gather studies.

Soon the second semester was about to start. Our tuitions started earlier than our schools. November was the month for our reunion-all friends together again, all pranks would be again repeated and the examination tensions will again reveal. But the most important of all watching Rehan and simply staring at his cute face and enjoying the moment were above all.

IT WAS JUST ABOUT TO BEGIN AGAIN!!!

SIX

"How were the vacations, babe?" Dharti said to me in **an exciting voice.**

"The most memorable and enjoying. How were yours?" I said in a pale voice.

"As usual I just visited village", she replied looking down and then we simply stared at each other and burst out into a small laughter.

"Where's he?" I thought to myself, looking through my eyes here-and-there and my mind glued with one thought-"What would he be wearing today?"

We were standing into a group down the stairs in the complex. All were discussing about the vacations-How did it go? What did they do? Where did they go? What did they buy? Etc. etc.

Some had boring ones and some had exciting ones. It's always a perfect girl's talk when they meet after a couple of days. My mind was somewhere else with me only shaking my head saying a "yes" to whatever I was asked to. My eyes catched a glance of someone who walked in with a simple tomato red colored t-shirt with black jeans and the same red framed spectacles.

"OMG! It's Rehan" I whispered to myself having a sense of satisfaction in my mind and not changing my reaction to others and simply smiling at no reason but with a limit on my face.

It seemed as if I was given something which I wanted since a decade. We went upstairs at 7 p.m. for our chemistry class and sat at the usual place we sat.

"Did he see me?" I thought and was talking with Tannie about the topic which was going on in the class.

"What is the molecular formula for sulphuric acid and how can we write it in such equations?" Tannie asked me in a confused voice.

Tannie hated chemistry as it seemed to be quite boring for her and she said she loved not to study. I was just about to answer her question when I saw Rehan looking at me.

I as if I knew nothing acted like I was looking around and waved my eyes at him. He with a sudden swift looked down and had a slight smile on his face.

"What was that? Did he just saw me? And smiled? ".

Questions rolled down my mind and I was just silly to answer any of them. The classes got over and I went home. I wanted to talk to Dharti about my attraction towards Rehan the next day. As she was my best friend, I decided to tell her about the things which were happening to me since a last few months.

We were sitting at the canteen which was near the parking area of our school and it was recess-time and we both were alone waiting for the others to come.

"I like a boy from our tuition", I said in a simple manner.

"Who? How does he look like? What is his name? Do you know him? Do I know him? Tell me" Questions started bursting on me as a loom cracker burst.

"Whoa! Wait a sec. So many questions at a time", I replied laughing.

"Then say who's he?" she again asked excitedly.

"His name is Rehan. He studies in the class with Mugdha at her school. He comes at our physics and chemistry class same batch. And I don't know much about him." I said simply.

"So it's the boy you once showed me besides the blue t-shirt-one?"

"Yes"

"Good choice. Handsomest!!" She said teasing me.

Actually teasing her was the best part I ever do every day. She too had a crush on someone who was from "ST.Xaviers". Dharti was a little crazy about the guy Karan who used to come to our physics class with us. Usually I used to call her "KK" as it matched with the initials of her crush's name.

Soon we headed off to class after our recess as it was our chemistry lab.

The next day at the tuition's we had our chemistry class.

"Had you prepared anything?" Tanvi asked me.

"Yes dear!"

Here it is Tanvi. Tanvi Shirke, a Marathi girl who was my Chemistry tuition friend and we usually met up at our AIEEE classes. She was a math-student like me, a fun loving girl and just the same as me as we both loved to talk a lot. Constant murmuring about any shit in this world was one of the things we did when we met. She too had a crush on someone who was just the opposite of her. But as usual crushes are crushes.

It was our chemistry AIEEE class and we had to go for a test. I, Mugdha, Natasha and Tanvi were the ones to go for the test. We all wore a white that day as we did most of the time.

We would decide which color clothes to wear. Maybe it seems funny but it's what we usually do. We went in the class, kept our bags at distant places and went down for snacks as Mugdha was hungry. Usually, we had to have our food in between the class's time as Sunday's were a full day scheduled. We had our lunch and went again to the class.

I went to my place where I kept my bag. I saw Rehan sitting on the same bench where I kept my bag. A numerous number of thoughts started running in my mind and I just simply went there. I looked at him and he looked at me.

We had a slight smile on our faces and I without saying anything took my bag and went and sat on the opposite bench.

"What did I just do? Why did I miss that chance sitting beside him?"

I was so angry at myself that I wanted someone to punch me on my face. Tanvi just gave a questioning face to me and it seems as if I did not have the guts to sit beside my crush. But it's alright. I said to my heart. It is the same feeling everyone has when they see their crushes.

> *"You are a powerful person when your presence is able to increase or decrease someone's heartbeat".*

It was my daddy's birthday and I was happy as Dad planned a dinner that night after my tuition. I wore my new orange colored plain kurti with folded sleeves.

My physics classes were going on. I was sitting at the left corner of the bench. Rehan was sitting behind me but a one bench leaving behind. I was playing with my blue colored F+U+N pencil when it slipped from my hands and fell down. When we were given a small break to study, I bent down and searched for my pencil.

"OH! God, it was near Rehan's left foot".

Now what?

I elbowed Dharti and asked her to Say Rehan to give the pencil back. Rehan knew it was mine and he was staring in front.

"Excuse me. Can you please give me that pencil?"

Rehan bent down took the pencil and lended it to Dharti.

"Thank-you", Dharti said.

"You're welcome!"

I was simply looking at the pages of my physics textbook but my ears concentrated on what was happening between Dharti and Rehan.

"Here's your pencil!", Dharti giggled and gave me my pencil in front of Rehan.

*   *   *

It was our physics class and we were on the topic of "Superconductors and its properties". I was paying attention to the lecture carefully as I had a test on the respective topic the next weekend. Rehan sat the bench leaving one behind me. He was not completely visible but I could only see his green and black and white checks sleeve of his shirt. He was playing with his orange F+U+N pencil in his hand and paying attention to the lecture.

The pencil slipped and came near my leg rolling. I saw it but did not give a reaction.

"Excuse me!" a voice came from behind.

Dharti looked back.

"Can I get my pencil? It has fallen near her leg", Rehan said pointing towards the ground.

I simply smiled looking down. Dharti called me. I looked at her. And she pointed towards the pencil and then pointing towards Rehan and said "PENCIL".

I acted as if I knew nothing. Bent down and turned behind and lended him his pencil. He was looking at me. And I was not looking at him.

"Thank-you", he said but I turned in front.

I paused for a second again turned back. He was still looking.

"Welcome", I replied with a smile.

He smiled too and I turned in front.

SEVEN

It was January and I always loved when that month arrived. It was my birthday month. I am always excited for my birthdays usually a month before. Surprises, gifts, parties and celebrations-makes that day special.

Nevertheless, it was 25th and 3 days were left for my birthday to come. I went shopping all around the city to find an outfit for my birthday. At last I found a Yellow-colored Thin T-shirt with black buttons in front and a Dark-yellow belt in the bottom of it. The main reason to buy that T-shirt was the color behind it. "Yellow" was it. My favorite Color. I was excited for the day to come and then it arrived.

At the midnight, my phone rang;

"You're my pumpkin, pumpkin,
Hello honey bunny.
I'm you're dumpling dumpling,
Hello honey bunny."

I woke up from my slumber and picked up the call. It was of Mugdha.

"Happy Birthday to you, Happy Birthday to you…." she sang in a pleasant voice.

I was so happy to hear it from her. I thanked her and hung up the call. Two minutes later my phone buzzed again. This time it was Tanvi.

"Happy Birthday Mayra. Have a great day", she said excitedly. Her sister Krishna also wished me. She wished Natasha also. As I and Natasha were twins I had to share my birthday with her and it was a pleasure doing that.

We both thanked Tanvi and slept again. The phone rang that night till 3a.m. and I thanked them all.

Next Morning I got up. My Mom woke me up by kissing my forehead. I looked at her with half eyes opened.

"Happy Birthday my jaan", she wished me with a great smile.

I hugged her and thanked her. She also wished Natasha. My Dad also wished both of us.

"We are the proud parents of two-Seventeen year old twins!" They said proudly to each other. At that moment I wished to pause it for some time and capture it forever. I had never seen my parents so happy earlier.

"MOTHER-The word itself shows how we females are reborn on the same day our child is born."

My mother was the happiest person I could ever have seen that day, happy more than me on my birthday. I got ready bowed in front of God-prayed for a happy and successful year ahead and went to school.

My friends wished me happy birthday. In fact everybody I met wished me and gave happy greetings. I wished that Rehan also wished me and hoped so. We had our assembly and we all stood together in a queue according to our heights.

Natasha was the first one followed by Jess and then Dharti. Behind her were Annie then Me and then Aaliya and Tannie. The hymn was sung and then a speech was given on "Army Day" as 28th January is celebrated as that day. My mind clanged to the hymn very strongly as it gives a few seconds of peace in mind.

"Ahh! What's so different in your birthday day?" I thought to myself. People just stare at you as if you're the one whose has the only birthday that day and everyone even your enemies maybe, wish you a great year ahead. Apparently the school went well and I headed off home.

It was the same routine not quite different from the daily days. But it felt special enough getting a year much older and growing elder. Yeah! I knew I was growing older and even getting closer to my dreams.

"The Alone-trip and visiting places of the world especially LOS ANGELES topping the to-travel list. Capturing funny selfies in front of the famous places round the globe and knowing different languages, people and their cultures.

Yeah! It was quite of fun. Maybe quite better than drinking alcohol and getting puked or maybe jumping from a high mountain and sky-diving.

The list also consisted of the deep-sea diving. Why not? Experience, the world down the waters. It is amazing. Indeed, very beautiful. Everyone should see that. The next was yeah! My house-terrace. 2 a.m.-early morning. On a full moon night with one sandwich and a glass of mock tail-with my "SPECIAL ONE"!"

As he also had to stroll on the beach on a full moon night listening to all the things I say to him.

This all funny yet interesting-of course for me! My birthday wishes-which I was going to fulfill every coming year of my Life! Alone!"

I reached home at one and a half hour, when my watch stroked... I got ready and had my lunch. Mom had cooked a special recipe for me and sister- It spelled like "Risotto Pasta"-A typical Italian cuisine. I was impressed for mumma cooking a meal for me. That seems special.

"Birthday's are indeed the day when the whole world makes you seem special right from the cake cutting part at midnight to the special surprises awaiting for the day!"

I completed my lunch quickly. Got ready and there was he. My driver called out for my tuitions. Yes, the time arrived for which I was waiting for. Watching Rehan. Yes, maybe!

My mathematics tuition got over quickly. And I reached there- my physics tuition as usual. I was dressed up in a simple yellow colored plain net t-shirt with small black buttons in front like forming a row and black jeans. I kept my hair untied just flowing in air when the winds came. Natasha wore a pink colored t-shirt with some lace-work in front near the neck and a long sleeve-black colored and blue jeans. She ponied her hair. Yes, we did not looked twins that day also as we don't look on either days! People often get mistook by us when they come to know that we are twins but they say,

"Please! Don't lie. You're not twins."

I mean. There is something like unidentical twins on this earth. Why does everyone behave so weird on the first look? It did not concern us. Yeah! Rehan-He wore a grey colored t-shirt. Long sleeves, his hair as usual covering up to his eyes and his red-framed spectacles.

He looked simply awesome! As that was the reason why my birthday looked special that Day! The reason behind why I was constantly smiling or maybe blushing that whole day!

At the end of the chemistry class, Mugdha, Tanvi and Viraj waited downstairs. They planned a surprise! We cut the cake-a chocolate cake with vanilla essence and cherries on the top of it! It was just beautiful. Everyone sang the Birthday song and we blew off the candles.

Rehan was standing a ten-foot away with Shivani. What on earth was she doing with him? They were giggling and laughing on some talk which they did. I mean come on Rehan; it was a special day for me. You ought not to spoil it. But no he wasn't. Because though he was talking to Shivani, his eyes were constantly glued at the celebration we were making!

The day was over and we all left for our respective home. It was the best birthday until now as someone's smile brought a smile on my face.

"Yes, Mayra! You're falling in Love. Maybe! Shut up, Stupid-Happy birthday once again!" I whispered to myself. Hugged my Teddy bear and went to deep slumber.

EIGHT

It was a Tuesday. We had our physics tuitions directly from our school. I changed my clothes at my Masi's place, which was nearer to my tuition. I had some lunch there and quickly went for the class. We were waiting on the first-floor stairs.

I, Dharti and Natasha were waiting for Aaliya to come. I and Dharti were having a jolly time when I ran after her trying to hit her. I just was about to slap her when I slapped someone else. I looked in amazement and a little bit of guilt. Dharti moved aside and I slapped a boy on his shoulder. He wore a pink and white checks shirt and the same red colored frame specs.

"OH! My God. It was Rehan"

I just did not give any look at him. He was also confused on what on earth was I doing. We just simply smiled at each other and went to the class. He went for his mathematics class and I went to the physics class. I just did not know what did I do and Dharti kept laughing all the while I gazed at her during the physics lecture. I kept thinking in my mind whether I should say sorry to Rehan for my act but come on, it was just an accident. But still my concentration level that does went down to 10% in the physics lecture that day.

Up to four or five days I did not look at Rehan thinking what would he be thinking of me-whether a screwed up idiot or something else. But its okay-I was too nervous to over think about that day.

Few days later during our chemistry class, Tanvi and Manu said they had planned a surprise for me today. I had no idea about what they were planning and I simply concentrated on my lecture and the place where Rehan was sitting.

The class got over and we left for home. There was some quarrel going on between two boys downstairs. I was walking in front looking downstairs. Rehan was walking in front of me. Manu went to him, stopped him and asked,

"Do you like Mayra?"

I heard that and paused for a moment. My attention from watching the quarrel got disturbed. I just simply looked at Rehan in surprise when he too was staring at me.

"No, no, no, Rehan! I knew nothing about It.", I whispered to myself when he said.

"No, I don't like her."

Those words were like someone stabbing a sharp pointed dagger onto my chest. He just looked at me and went away climbing the stairs downwards. I wished I could erase the last few moments from my life. I just angrily went up to Tanvi, Manu and Natasha who stood smiling there.

"What did you people just do? Is this your surprise?"

"Yes", mumbled Tanvi.

"You know I hate such things. Why did you just do that? I am not going to talk with the three of you for your crazy, pathetic surprise."

I said and went angrily down. They shouted to call me back but I went. Rehan stood downstairs. I did not look at him and just went and sat in my rickshaw waiting for Natasha to come. And we went home.

For some days I did not look at Rehan. I thought maybe it was quite silly but that was how I was. The weekends had the physics test and I was all into the preparations for it. It was a 70-mark test covering 6 chapters from the course.

We went and sat at the places allocated by the invigilator on the test day. The place in front of me was empty and I sat on the third last bench. The test started. I was busy in reading the multiple choice questions part-A from my question paper when someone walked in the class.

"Here sit here!" the invigilator pointed to the place in front of me.

It was Rehan. I looked up. We had an eye contact and I again looked down into my paper acting as if I did not care whether it was him or someone else. My fingers touched him more than ten times that day. Every time he would lean to sit back his back would touch my fingers or my question paper would get stuck up into his back.

I heard a "SORRY" ten or maybe more from his mouth that day. I did not want that but every time he said that it always appeared cute to me.

What was going on? I did not know. I loved to visit the tuitions, to wait for them after schools. It was just a different feeling when you wait for someone to come and when he comes you just act as if you don't know he has arrived.

The last few days of March ended up in daily tests. We were allotted with time-tables of different tests for all the three subjects with each day and covering almost all the syllabus three-to-four times.

It was 24th of March and it was quite an important day for me as a I was having my physics exam at tuition. It was a 70 mark exam covering almost all the important chapters from the syllabus. I waited for Dharti when I reached the complex just a few minutes earlier the test. My Mom came to drop me that day. I was standing with my mom waiting for Dharti and Aal along with Natasha. At that time Rehan passed by and went upstairs.

I looked at him and gave a slight smile not catching my mother's glimpse. Pretending nothing happened I just continued talking with my mother but having my mind indulged somewhere else. Dharti arrived a few minutes later and we went up for the class. Aal and Natasha sat on the second last bench as suggested by the invigilator.

"Mayra, come here and sit in the middle between these two." the invigilator said to me pointing towards an empty place.

Rehan was sitting on the respective bench where the invigilator said to me to sit. I went ahead and sat there acting as if I did not care about that Rehan was going to sit exactly besides me for the next three hours. It struck 1:30p.m. And the papers were distributed.

I started to mark the mcq's which I knew and acted as if I did not care about who was sitting beside me. But inside my heart, my world turned tipsy-topsy with every glimpse of Rehan seeing me write my paper. I would look at him with my eyes slanted so that I could see him from a closer view. He was looking perfect in his tight buttoned-black shirt and his red specs. Butterflies rolled around in my stomach. But I still concentrated on my paper.

I was writing when Rehan raised his hand for an extra supplementary. The invigilator came and gave the supplementary to me and I passed it to him without looking at him. After some time.

"Excuse me", Rehan said to me in a polite manner.

Firstly I did not pay my attention and continued to write my paper.

"Excuse me", he said again with the same polite manner.

I looked at him and gave a questioning face to him thinking "YES" in my mind. I smiled at him and he too smiled back.

"I need a pencil. Can you borrow yours with me?" he asked me.

"Yes! Of course", I said to him and gave him my red color nip pencil which I held I my left hand while writing my paper.

Ten minutes were left for the paper to complete. I almost checked my answers and stapled my supplementary and packed up my bag. I looked at Rehan and he had held my pencil in his left hand busy solving the numerical on his calculator. I looked at him and said.

"Excuse me."

He did not give a response. I again said it and he looked at me. We had an eye-contact and I pointed towards my pencil. He gave me the pencil and said.

"THANK-YOU".

I did not give a response and stood up wearing my bag on my shoulders. I then turned to him and he looked at me. I smiled at him and said.

"WELCOME"

He looked at me and smiled. And I left the class.

NINE

It was 15th of April. We had a holiday at tuition as we had our vacation as our exams were completed for the second semester. I was at my uncle's place when my phone rang "TRING-TRING" and I received Dharti's call around 4 in the evening.

DHARTI-"Hello"

MAYRA-"Haan bol"

DHARTI-"Do u know aaje shu che?" ☺

MAYRA-"Shu?" :O

DHARTI-"Aaje Rehan ni b'day che. Idiot." ☺☺☺

MAYRA-"What? Seriously? How did you know? Kevi te khabar tane? Bolne"

DHARTI-"I checked it on my facebook page. I got a notification saying.

"IT IS REHAN SONI'S BIRTHDAY TODAY""☺☺☺

MAYRA-"Ohhh! Dharti. This is the best thing you have ever told me."☺☺☺☺☺☺☺

At that very moment I got so excited for a few seconds. It was the birthday of the person I had a big fat crush on and I came to know it in the evening. This is so not fair I couldn't even wish him. ☹☹☹☹☹

The next day our third semester tuitions began and we all were back. I was glad as I could at least see Rehan though not able to wish him on his birthday.

Few days later, a Saturday it turned up to be very hectic as we had our first physics test at tuitions consisting of the third semester syllabus and of 70 marks. Rehan turns up to give his test in the earlier batch and I got to give it in the second batch. So we did not give the tests in the same batches.

I wanted to eagerly see him and so I just said to Dharti to do something.

"Wait! Let's call him…" said Dharti excitingly.

"What?" I questioned surprisingly.

"And how so?"

"Speak his number", she said swiftly opening the dialing keypad on Heena's cell phone.

"Nine Nine five eight…………" I spoke the complete number.

TRING TRING TRING TRING TRING TRING.
. . .

The phone rang thrice and then it was answered from the other side.

"Hello", said Rehan.

"Hello"

"Who's this???"

"This is REHAN"

"Who are you???"

Dharti got confused. It was all happening too fast and we were not getting to understand what to speak. Rehan on the other side kept on asking who it was. At that moment I saw a stitching shop in front of the place we stood. It read "KAMLA STICHING CENTER". I mimicries to Dharti and told her to speak "Kamlaben" to Rehan.

> "Hello. I Kamlaben"
> Rehan was bewildered.
> "Sorry, wrong number."

And he hanged up the call. I heard the whole conversation as the phone was on speaker all throughout the call. It was a little silly to speak a name which spelt a little horrible to him.

But love is a roller-coaster ride. It takes you up and down and makes you do silly things which you'll pretend you haven't done.

TEN

Few days later Dharti send a message to Rehan on his face book Id.

"Happy birthday Rehan...........................From Mayra"

He replied-"TQ"

I just shouted on Dharti for this pathetic thing. Because I did not wanted Rehan to know about what I felt for him and also several thoughts rolled around in my mind.

"What would he be thinking? Why did Dharti wish him like that? Would he ever talk to me? Etc etc etc"

I was at my grandparent's home. It was a typical Sunday-a boring day as usual Sundays as I did not have tuitions and I did not have to go out of home and stay at my place sitting in front of the television screen, eating popcorns and French-fries with extra ketch-up.

I wanted to hear Rehan's voice. I went to the kitchen and helped my aunt in some household work. She looked at me and said,

"You seemed to be upset. What happened?"

I told her about my wish to hear his voice. She brought her mobile and told me to dial Rehan's number. I looked at her in amazement and she said,

"C'mon go ahead!"

I dialed Rehan's number and the phone rang. She kept the phone on speaker and told me to Sshhh.

"Hello"

"Hello, who's this?"

"This is Rehan and who are you?"

"This is Yoginiben. And where are you speaking from?"

"I'm speaking from Surat! Whom do you need?"

"I need Kamleshbhai"

"Sorry! Wrong number"

And he hanged up the phone. I could hear his voice for 7 odd minutes and that made my day. I just hugged my aunt in excitement. But this time too we made a mistake by saying a weird name in front of him. I don't get why it is always Rehan when I need to spell such names. : P

It was evening and we had our physics classes. I went up to the class and sat at the respective place. A boy walked in who seemed to be known to me. He reminded me of someone and I started to think by myself whether who was he? Then I ran my brain and God! I was such a fool. It was Rehan without his red-framed spectacles. He was looking the handsomest of all the boys present there to me. He looked the cutest without specs.

His grey-colored t-shirt, hair coming and touching his eye-lids perfectly made him the cutest.

That class sir made an important announcement after the class got over. The third semester was about to begin in the next month.

"All the students who have their schools leaving at 12:15 p.m. will be allotted the first batch and the students whose schools leave at 12:30 will be allotted the second batch."

That meant I and Rehan had different batches from now onwards. This can't be possible. Life can't be so cruel.

I just thought to myself for two seconds that if I could erase the words Sir said two minutes back. But nothing was into my hands and I had to follow the schedule as formatted. That meant that I would be able to see Rehan only during tests at the weekends or during some combined classes.

Dharti knew everything about me and Rehan and she even insisted sometimes not to be so much involved into this as it was a possibility for me to get hurt in the coming future. But love has no limit.

Things were getting darker between me and her. I did not get a strong feeling for our friendship anymore. Though we used to be on each other's side the all time, things seems=d to be a little changed.

I just wanted to go and hug my best friend and cry to her about my sadness. But she said that I was childish and immature about such things and used to cry on silly little issues.

But the fact was "NO MATTER HOW MUCH YOU CRY, IF YOU'RE CLOSE TO ANYONE HE WILL SEE YOUR PAIN AND WILL TRY TO CONVINCE YOU"

I did not get to know what was happening but there was something between us which I was not able to understand. Our group was on the verge of some separation. And the blame was given to me. It was me who was childish, it was me who was immature, it was me who did not understood anything. And I thought that I was surrounded with the people who understand me the most.

ELEVEN

Tannie, Dharti and Aal behaved a little different than before. I did not know the perfect reason for that.

It was our chemistry exam directly after the school and we were seated at the physics class. Tannie, Aal and Natasha sat in the left side of the class benches while I and Dharti sat on the right side.

I was not able to see Rehan that day as we arrived quite late that day.

I was very hungry after the class and decided to go at some place to eat. I asked all the others to accompany me.

Tannie was not in a good mood that day as her face clearly depicted some sort of rude behavior or maybe ignorance. She called up her mom and ordered three dishes.

My mind startled up with weird thoughts and I asked her.

"Why did you order three when we are five?"

"I ordered for Aal, Dharti and me."

She knew Natasha was not hungry. And I was yelling on the top of my noise. It was noon time and none of the restaurants were open except a coffee shop. But drinking a coffee in such hot climate would not end up my starvation.

I felt really bad on such an action of Tannie. And I ended up eating nothing that day and went directly to my home after that.

The worst days were starting and I was not so happy. Friendships were on the verge of division. Things started getting bitter after that day. Finally 10th June arrived when the first class without Rehan was about to begin.

I was sitting next to Tanvi in chemistry class when Dharti arrived with Aal. They both went and sat on the first bench.

"The person whom I used to share every small thing of my life did not even bother to look at me today"

WHEN YOU LOSE SOMEONE WHO IS VERY DEAR TO YOU,
IT HITS YOU…
ALL THE CHANCES YOU DID NOT TAKE,
ALL THE THINGS YOU DID NOT SAY,
BECAUSE THE TRUTH IS THAT YOU THINK YOU HAVE IT FOREVER, BUT YOU DON'T……………YOU NEVER DO!

Twenty days later it was the first Sunday after the classed were departed. I was as happy at that day as we were going to have our JEE classes. Finally a class with Rehan after so many days of despair and separation. God finally got us a day together again in his calendar to make me happy. ☺

I and Tanvi were sitting near the last benches about the last fourth bench from behind. At that time someone in yellow colored strips t-shirt entered into the class and sat just on the opposite bench row of my row. I did not know Rehan had come into the class. Instead I was busy playing with Tanvi-we were busy playing....she took out the clip from my hair due to which strands of hair started to fall on my face. It was irritating me and so I asked her to give it back but every time I would lean forward towards her to take my clip. She would step back and take her arms backside so I would miss the clip again. Then we would pause for a minute then look at each other and laugh loudly.

This happened for four-to-five times until I got my clip back. I did not know Rehan was noticing us. But when we stopped our stupidity when sir entered the class for the lecture to precede Mugdha told me.

"Mayuu, do you know what?"

"What Dha?"

"Rehan was continuously watching you when you were playing with Tanvi and there was a continuous smile on his face."

"Seriously?"

"Yes babe!"

I got a chill in my stomach. Butterflies were running in my stomach and I was almost to the peak thinking about weird situations in my mind.

TWELVE

I was late at the tuition that day. I and Dharti were running when I saw Rehan talking with Anaya. They were standing on the left most corners of the stairs where other friends were sitting on the swing and talking. I did not give a look, just looking downwards and went upstairs.

I just wanted to go and kill Anaya at that very moment. In the whole world she got only Rehan to talk with. But weirdness cracked my mind when thoughts came to my mind- Why I was jealous? Should I go and also talk with him too? Why did I feel so shy?

I looked at Dharti and gave a weird face mimicking the same way Anaya was talking with Rehan. She started laughing loudly and insisted me to move to the class.

"Why on earth does every girl come and talk with Rehan??"

I was thinking about it the whole time. Not knowing what to do? First of all I was the person who was shy enough to go and talk with the person I loved at that very moment and secondly I got jealous enough when he talks with any random girl.

I was busy scrolling down through the timeline of my face book profile.

"I need to add friends"

I went to the "Find Friends" option and started scrolling down to the random names appearing on my mobile screen.

Dharti Patel- ADD
Natasha Kashyap- ADD
Anjie Shukla- ADD
Annie Fernando- ADD
Anaya Patel- NO
Ayushi Sinhala- NO
Dhruv Shah- ADD
Vatsal Patel- ADD
Jess Cesar- ADD
Jatin Desai- ADD

My phone got hang when I constantly was tapping the screen to add the members to my friend-list. I was getting frustrated and I tried to switch it off but there was no result.

An hour later my phone came to its normal position when the music beeped I suddenly woke up from my slumber and immediately logged in to my face book account.

I opened the homepage when I saw a notification.

"YOU POKED REHAN SONI"

My eyes remained still on my mobile screen and I was not knowing how to response. All I thought was how would be Rehan's reaction when he would come to know I poked him. I Remembered Anjie's word.

"Don't poke anyone while using your account"

When I was learning to use the account settings and working from her. I immediately called her. The phone rang and my nervousness was increasing more and more.

Hello"

"Hey "Anjie"

"I needed your help"

"Haa dear..... Bolo"

"Meri ek friend hai. Usne naya naya facebook use karna start kiya hai. Usne galati se ek unknown ko poke kar diya hai. Ab kya vo use unpoke kar sakti hai???"

"No dear...you can't unpoke someone"

"So now what should she do?"

"See you tell your friend to send a message to that unknown person that the poke was done by mistake... that's it"

"Okay! Dear thankyou so much"

"Welcome"

"Bubye dea"

"Byee"

I hanged up the phone and opened Rehan's profile. I went to his message box and typed a message:

"Sorry.........I poked you by mistake......I have touch screen cell and it got hanged.......sorry!"

I typed this much and pressed the send button. My heartbeats were almost audible which were beating as swiftly as the horse runs during a horse race.

The next morning I woke up with again some sorts of weird thoughts running down my mind. I took my bath and logged in my account. There was a new message in my inbox. It was of Rehan.

A bright smile came onto my face. Reading just a line from my inbox-"You have a message from REHAN SONI" made my day. The reply was "It's OK......!" I thought should I reply or not and typed "Ty...☺" and pressed the sent button.

The boring reply was "wc" not even a smiley: P

THIRTEEN

The tuitions were combined on the 28th of September and so there was a large rush in our batch. It was 6:30 and we reached late to the class so we have to sit on the second last bench that day. I sat with Mugdha outside and Natasha sat with Tanvi.

It was 6:35 and still Rehan was not in sight. I thought he would not come to the tuition that day when at 6:37 he entered the class and sat exactly on the last bench behind us.

As soon as he sat behind us, Mugdha, Tanvi and Natasha started teasing me. They started to shout my name loudly so that it maybe audible to Rehan and I was just acting I did not listen to them and was busy solving my assignments.

At that moment Sir distributed new assignments to the whole class for the covering of the next chapter. Due to more students in the class that day, there was shortage of assignment papers and so we had to share with the last bench students also.

Mugdha and Tanvi started their prank again and would ask me "Do you need the assignment, Mayera?"

"Or should we give it back?"

I snatched the assignment from their hand saying nothing and started reading the notes provided on the first page of it. The chapter was "Magnetism"

The explanation was written in Hindi. I showed it to Mugdha and she started giggling on seeing it. We both read the lines written in it which read "Chumbakiya shetra" means "magnetic field".

On reading it we started laughing looking at each other when Jaswant who was sitting behind asked us for the assignment as he wanted to refer the theory.

He also started laughing on seeing the explanation in Hindi and showed it to Rehan. Rehan started reading and he also read the same thing "Chumbakiya shetra"

Mugdha, Tanvi and Natasha everybody looked at me and started laughing. I was just looking down not giving a reaction to their laugh. ☺

The two hour class atlast ended but the three of them did not stop teasing me.

The classes were now conducted less mostly on the Saturday's and Sunday's as the exams were near. So the JEE classes were only conducted.

The board exams dates were out and all were busy in the preparation of the exam. I again got the board center in my own school as the first and the second semester.

I was happy as Rehan was also in the same school. I told Mugdha to confirm his board exam center when she would go to collect the hall ticket from her school.

The exams got over and the year was about to end. The fourth semester just passed away in a blink of the eye. I wanted to hold the moments like the sand in my fist. But I knew it was slipping right through my hands and I was not able to do anything. I did not have the odesity to go and talk with the person I loved.

Was it fear? Or shyness? Or something else?

The last month arrived when our 12th was going to end. Our last semester examination was over and we did not have to attend the regular classes anymore.

"No more leaning on the railing bars and waiting for Rehan to come.

No more bunks with all the people who were dearer to me.

No more teasing me with Rehan.

No more seeing Rehan sitting on the opposite bench and just waiting from him to smile.

No more canteen food-No more fights-No more special memories"

Everything was going to go and a new life would start. The greatest fear I have was:

"Would I ever talk to Rehan in my life?"

2nd April. It was the last day of our JEE Chemistry class. As we had our JEE paper on 6th April, our sir decided to conduct a last class for the quick revision. I, Mariya and Natasha were sitting together talking with other girls who were busy discussing the same topic-"What after 12th?"

My mind was all stuck up on one person who was Rehan and he was not in my sight. When I turned backwards and saw him sitting with Vatsal in a black and grey checks shirt and his same yellow framed spectacles. He had the same innocent face which he had on the day I first saw him.

I just was looking at him and he was busy solving the assignment sir provided us in the last class. The watch struck 2:30 p.m. and the class completed.

The last class of my 12th standard completed. I looked at everybody present there. I was not sure if I was going to see any of these people again in my life after some time. I was not sure if I was going to see Rehan after that day.

I stood there on the third floor of my tuition building when I saw Rehan unparking his vehicle and heading off to his home. I stay still, quietly looking at him and he put on the keys of the vehicle and accelerated, took a turn and went away. He soon faded and was not visible on the end of the road. HE HAD GONE............

I too hugged Mariya and we all headed off to home. I sat in my rickshaw and went home.

FOURTEEN

The vacations started and I had nothing to do at home except to watch the daily soaps along with my grandmother. I decided to join programming language tuition so that it would be a help to me in my future.

The tuition was a 2 or a 3 kilometer away from my home. It was just a walking distance so I, Natasha and my cousin Mahek used to go everyday there together.

It was like refreshment from the boring schedule at home. And even we could sometimes get a chance to bunk the class and go to eat somewhere. Maybe that was few of our last bunks of school-life.

I was accompanied with my school friend Simran and Nami over there too. It was just like a recalling of our school days, remembering all the good-joyful-bitter-sad days which were written by the pen called school-life and about which the chapters were going to end soon.

I was returning home with my rickshaw-wala. As I had to stay at my grandmother's house, Mom instructed me and Natasha to go by rickshaw. I was busy listening to the songs played in my playlist and seeing through the streets silently when my phone beeped. It was a watsapp message from an unknown number.

"Hi"

I analyzed the number to see if it belonged to any of my contact list but it did not. Before replying I asked Natasha to check the true caller and see to who did the number belonged to.

"Abhi Soni"

The true caller app showed. I was a little confused on seeing the name first as the first thought which came up to my mind was the surname- "SONI". Thoughts started rolling down whether did he have any connection with Rehan? But it was two months since the tuitions got over and I did not think it would be someone mutually in friends with Rehan. Just at the second moment another message popped up by the same unknown number.

ABHI-"Hi, I'm your new friend Abhi"

ME-"I don't have a friend name Abhi. Who are you??"

ABHI-"I'm Abhi Patel"

ME-"Are you sure?"

ABHI-"Okay okay! I'm Abhi Soni"

ME-"Then why did you say Patel?"

ABHI-"Just like that"

ME-"From where did you get this number?"

ABHI-"Doesn't matter. I want to be friends with you. Will you be?

ME-"I don't know you and I don't talk with the strangers"

ABHI-"That is what I want to tell you. We can be
    good friends and we may know each other also."
ME-"I have no interest in talking with you."

And so I stopped the conversation and blocked
the number from my watsapp account. I reached
home but was thinking about it all the time. Whether
really Abhi had some connection with Rehan? Or
how did he get my number?

I logged in my face book account and typed "Abhi
Soni" in the search list. There was one Abhi Soni
with the same profile picture-the one I had of that
unknown number which I received that evening. I
saw to the friend's section-2 mutual friends-out of
which one was "Aftab Marafatia", a tuition friend
of mine and the second name was "REHAN SONI".
My doubts were getting clearer and I had a strong
feeling that Abhi was somehow connected with
Rehan. I was nervous from outside but inside I too
was excited that at least after two months I got some
sort of hope about Rehan.

I was watching TV along with my brother after
completing my dinner. My phone ranged. It was 9:30
p.m. and the call was from an unknown number.
I received the call and it was "ABHI SONI". I got
scared at the first time when I listened to his voice
introducing me about him and telling me that he was
Abhi. I walked out of my room and closed the door
so that my brother would not see me talking on the
phone late night.

"I do not want to talk with you neither do I want to keep this friendship. Please understand"

"I do not want to panic you. I'm a simple guy and I just want you to be good friends with me", he said calming me down.

"How did you get this number?"

"I bought a new simcard from the company center. And I got your number from the simcard itself", he said to me.

"Are you making a fool of me here? Which company does give ready phone numbers in a simcard?"

"Exactly. But this is the truth. I got your number along some of the other 4-5 numbers in my simcard"

I did not believe him and hanged up the call by saying that I did not believe his words and still did not want to keep the friendship. He promised me to be good at first and if I did not wish to keep the friendship anymore I may block him.

I accepted as he said as it was getting late and he hanged up the call. The next day I received his call again. I completely analyzed his face book profile before talking to him and decided to ask him about Rehan also.

The very same day I asked one of my friend who was a mutual friend of me and Rehan too ask Rehan whether he knew Abhi or not. Rehan told my friend that he was his cousin-his uncle's son who stayed right beside his house.

I had the answer but still I asked Abhi how he knew Rehan. First of all he denied my question by saying he did not knew anyone by that name. But then on my forcing him he said that he was his far away relative. Abhi started becoming friendlier with me as well as my sister Natasha and so we started having a good bond of friendship.

We started coming to know each other and also started gossiping about idiotic jokes. We made a group on watsapp so that we could sometimes have funny conversations to spend some quality time.

FIFTEEN

Abhi became good friends with me and Natasha. So I asked Natasha to ask him about Rehan. On more insisting of Natasha to Abhi he decided to help us be friends with Rehan. He added Rehan to the watsapp group we already had. And so Rehan also started to talk in the group.

I was going through the timeline of my face book account when I got a message "Rehan Soni". I was still for two minutes on seeing the message from him. I thought to myself if I should reply or not? I shouted on the top of my voice.

I was not able to think anything. He messaged me on my watsapp but I replied him on messenger. As I did not open watsapp late night as my mother would ask me a hundred of questions why was my watsapp ON late night? : P

He immediately replied on messenger and we had a small conversation. He asked me how I and Abhi became friends. And he also asked me about a movie plan which Abhi planned for the four of us. But going for a movie would not be possible as my parents would not allow me.

So I denied Rehan for not coming for the movie. He asked me the reason for it but I just told him that it was due to a personal problem.

Then he started talking about his past few times. That he studied in the science stream and etc.

"You're free now?"

He asked me after sometime. I replied by saying a yes.

"Can I call you?"

I looked at the text of his and remained still for some time.

"Right now?"

"Yes"

"Okay"

"Wait 5 min"

And he logged off from the chat. I waited for him to call me and after sometime my phone ranged. It was Rehan. My heartbeats were almost beating heavily and I was not able to understand what I should say. I just decided to talk casually as if I'm talking to a close friend of mine and very easily.

"Hello", he said in the cutest voice.

"Hello, Hey Rehan"

I was feeling so special at that moment of the time as I was talking to the person who meant so much to me. And I did not imagine in my dreams that I would ever get to talk with him.

"What are you doing?"

"Nothing much watching TV"

"And you?"

"Same TV"

"What?"

"36 chambers of Shaolin"

"Good"

The conversation continued and I did not realize the time. It was 11:00 in the clock and I still was talking with him. We almost talked about many things from our tuition life to other things which we were going to decide for our future.

After sometime he asked me for Natasha. I said she was listening songs on her phone. He asked me to give the phone to her. I gave the phone to Natasha and slept beside her on my bed. I was listening to their talk but was not able to get anything.

They were talking and their talk continued for about more half an hour. At a time Rehan,

"I liked you but not her during tuitions and this is the truth"

I remained calmed for two minutes without thinking what did I just heard from the person whom I loved so much. There was nothing for me to hear and I just turned my side, put on my blanket, not seeing whether if they are still talking or not lay there.

My mind started to emerge with several thoughts out of which the first one was,

"All through these two years, the person whom I was crazy about likes my sister"

Thinking about all these, I tried to close my eyes when a drop of tear slipped through my right cheek. I tried to stop it but my hands lay stiff not wanting to move. I just wanted to hug someone so tightly-the best day of my life became the worst day.

The happiness turned into pages of sadness where I was not even permitted to do anything. Natasha came to me and just kissed my forehead.

"Don't worry! I'll never do anything wrong to you. I know you love him"

I tried to smile through my tearful face and said her goodnight. The sleepless night ended and my aunty came to wake me up. I was not having any idea what happened last night.

I just wanted to run away somewhere and scream on the top of my voice and asked God what did I do? That he even did not let me have one memorable day with Rehan. I plugged my earphones in and tried to sleep.

> *"Kahin toh, hogi woh, duniya jahan tu mere saath ho,*
> *Jahan mei, Jahan tu, aur jahan bas tere mere jasbat hai,*
> *Hogi jahan subha teri palko ki kirano mein,*
> *Loori jahan chand ki sune teri bahon mein,*
> *Jane na kahan vo duniya hai,*
> *Jane na vo hai bhi ya nahi?*
> *Jahan meri zindagi mujse itni khafa nahi."*

Hoping for Rehan was like holding the sand into my fist which gradually keeps on slipping.

"I wish that you get enough of the sun,

To keep up your bright attitude no matter how grey the days are.

I wish that you get enough of the rain,

To appreciate the sun even more darker.

I wish that you get enough happiness,

To keep up you in high spirits and an everlasting life.

I wish that you get enough pain,

To make you understand that even the smallest joys may appear the biggest.

I wish that you get enough gain,

To satisfy yourself whatever you want.

I wish that you get enough of loss,

To appreciate the things that you possess.

I wish that you get enough Hello's,

To get you through the final goodbye."

SIXTEEN

"Come your lunch is ready"

Mu aunt shouted from the kitchen and I and Natasha went for lunch. I did not wanted to react to the things happened and whatever Rehan said to Natasha about her and him.

I did not want to have cold wars between us. It was a Sunday so I as usual stayed at my nana's home. There were no tuitions. Abhi, I and Natasha were playing Antakshari on watsapp: P

Rehan did not chat but we three were in a mood to enjoy. Abhi knew what Rehan said last night and he also knew that I liked him. So he was cracking funny jokes which made a joyful environment in playing the game. The game continued when Abhi put forward a plan to meet.

"Let's the four of us meet somewhere"

I was not in a mood to meet Rehan after that. But Abhi insisted a lot so I said okay. We were making a plan to meet somewhere. Maybe after the busy schedule of our college lives we may meet or not. We decided to go at the Dumas beach away from the city rush. But it was not yet fixed. Rehan was unaware of the meeting yet.

After sometime my phone beeped. I went near the table, unplugged the charging plug and opened the inbox. It was Rehan, he was asking about the plan. I texted him after sometime even though I read the message long back: P

We had a small conversation in which he asked me about how we're going to meet and when. At last it was decided that we would meet on the tenth of June.

I was very excited as it was finally that God listened to my prayers and gave me a chance to talk with Rehan face-to-face no matter he loved someone else. At least I would get a chance to look at the love of my life-maybe for the last time but not the least.

The day finally arrived. All over from morning I was waiting for my watch to struck 3:30 p.m. At 3 I started dressing up myself.

I put on a loose pink and white stripped t-shirt with plain color and bordered lace. I decided to plait my hair and asked Natasha to put me on a new hairstyle which would make me look different from the other days Rehan had been seeing me. I simply kept my eyes plain with a brush of liner on my top of eye-lashes and looked myself in the mirror. I seemed to be the happiest girl at that moment that was going to bunk my class for someone I loved since last a year.

"Please hurry up. We'll get late", I asked Natasha.

My brother Mahek also knew about our plan and he decided to go to his friend's home nearby which was at a walking distance from our tuition. Rehan called me up when I was going downstairs after telling my mom that we would get a little late that day as we had to do some extra sums.

We crossed the main road and then the street opposite it. We took the turn and came on the path our tuition was. My heartbeats were getting faster and beating heavily as soon as I saw Abhi and Rehan standing on the opposite side with their own vehicles.

Abhi came on in his black pulsar and Rehan on his blue colored DIO. Abhi and Natasha already decided that they would make the best meeting for me and Rehan. That is why Natasha ran ahead and sat behind Abhi. I denied to sit with Rehan but did not have any other option. I put my hand on his right shoulder and sat behind him. He was just looking perfect in his blue and white colored stripped shirt-the one which he wore on last Rakshabandhan festival. I kept my bag between us so that a distance might be there between the two of us.

I put my earphones on so that I did not have to talk to him. Because I knew that as soon as I would talk to him I would reply something very silly. He asked me to put on my duppatta but as I did not like it, I kept it as it is.

When we were crossing the main road, I saw my uncle standing on the opposite side of the street. I just held Rehan hardly and bent down so that he may not see me. Rehan got confused why was I doing that but then we moved ahead and I explained to him and apologized. I was scared at that very moment whether someone does not catch us and the three of them made fun of me by commenting different sentences.

"Drop her here only and we will go", Rehan said to Abhi

When we were crossing the path near Udhna, Rehan's uncle crossed us. He saw us but gave a wicked smile to Rehan. As we were being seen by many of our relatives, Rehan and Abhi decided to take their car. They dropped me and Natasha near a temple and asked us to wait for five to ten minutes. Then he came with a red color NANO Car.

Abhi was driving and Rehan was sitting on the front seat beside him. We sat inside. Natasha behind Abhi and I behind Rehan. Then Abhi drove to Rehan's flat which was nearby. He drove by the wrong side so that we could reach there early.

We reached there and went to the fourth floor of the building by lift. The three of them were talking but I did not utter a word. I kept on playing game in my mobile listening to their talks and blushing by looking down.

SEVENTEEN

"There is no furnishing done to the house yet. So we will have to sit down", said Rehan looking at the three of us.

We all four sat down in the drawing room area. It was a nice beautiful flat with a drawing room, 2 bed rooms and a kitchen with a verandah and a temple area.

The drawing room had a big sliding window which would give a view of the society from there. We sat there and were talking about how did finally we had a day to meet.

"Snatch her phone. We are here to talk not play games", Abhi said to me giving me an angry look.

"But I don't want to talk"

"Why are you feeling shy because of Rehan here?"

"Ah! Why would I feel shy because of him?"

"As if everyone does not know over here that you have a soft corner for Rehan."

Everyone started teasing me and Rehan was just looking at me smiling as if he did not have to say anything after hearing to Natasha and Abhi. Then Rehan asked us for water and he went towards the kitchen to get some water.

Abhi and Natasha still continued to tease me and Rehan kept on blushing in the kitchen.

Then Abhi decided to give me and Rehan some privacy so that we could talk about something. We went to the left side bedroom.

Rehan asked me not to sit near the window as the neighbors would see and it would not look good. Natasha and Abhi went to the other room and they were just chilling out talking funny things which they did to make me and Rehan meet.

I and Rehan were all alone in that room and we were just sitting opposite to each other saying nothing. I kept starring on my mobile screen and he played with his jeans pocket button.

REHAN-"Don't be shy. It is okay if I know that you like me"

ME-"No I'm not shy. It's just I'm feeling a little awkward."

And this way our conversation started.

REHAN-"So from when does you like me?"

ME-"Me. I don't like you"

REHAN-"C'mon I know that you do. Not me everyone knew"

ME-"Second semester starting"

REHAN-"Oh! So why did you not talk with me at tuitions?"

ME-"You could also have taken the first step, Rehan"

REHAN-"Oh yeah ofc I could have."

He was not able to hear me and so he came and sat beside me. Exactly beside me. My heartbeats were rising and rising and I was blushing and blushing not thinking what he would think about me.

And thus we had a lot of talk like for almost an hour. We had a talk about our family members and also about our ex's, but hard luck for him-he was the first one whom I loved. We also talked about what we were planning to do after 12th.

The song which was running through my mind suited the moment very perfectly-It was-

> "Humko mili hai aaj yeh gadiyan naseeb se,
> Ji bhar ke dekh lijiye humko karib se,
> Phir aapke naseeb mein yeh baat ho na ho,
> Shayad phir iss janam mein mulakat ho na ho!"

At that time the light went and Rehan got up to see Abhi. He turned ON the switch but the power was cut. We decided to now proceed towards tuition as we would get late if we had stayed a little more.

We reached the street opposite to our tuition where Mahek was already waiting for us. I moved out of the car just looked at Rehan and stand still.

Abhi waved his hand biding us goodbye and drove the car. They went and the day ended.

Rehan had gone. I did not know whether I would get a chance to meet him again in my life again. Whether God would again show mercy on me to complete my incomplete love story. I went home got freshen up and looked at Shivji's picture hanged up on my bedroom wall.

"I Closed my eyes and joined my hands and thanked him heartily that he had at least let me expressed my words that I really loved him to the person which had gone maybe forever."

I went to bed remembering all the things which happened that day and had a smile on my face. Since Last two years it was the first day which I slept peacefully remembering Rehan with a smile on my face-with a ray of satisfaction.

"I wanted you to become someone whom I Loved,

I wanted to go back to the one I belonged,

You've got something I need,

In this world full of people,

There's only one killing me,

And if I die once,

I wish I could die with you,

But he never returned nor did he say how sorry he was,

I neither turned back, nor did I wait for an apology,

Least did I expect him to come AND say the words rest,

"Cause she knew", Unspoken heartfelt regrets are the best!!!"

3 MONTHS LATER.

EIGHTEEN

I shifted to Baroda city away from home. I was on the verge of starting a new life where there would be new experiences and new friends. I left Surat a long behind and there was only left were the memories which I gathered since the last sixteen years.

I was finally in my college life where I would have to become a little more mature and have contact with people by myself. There was no mom to wake me up early morning and ask me to get ready for college. Neither there was Dad all by my side to stay whenever I felt alone.

I did not have my grandmother who would cook me delicious food whenever I did not want to eat anything nor did I have my friends who were the supporting system to my life. They made my life complete. I had to make new friends and was all ready to experience a new phase of my life.

My hostel life was a very different chapter of my life as I had a very different experience in it. A room was allocated to me and Natasha who had 309 written on it.

This room belonged to us and we were the owner of it. It was the place where we would have to spend the next three years of our life. It was a simple room with two beds and two cupboards and two study tables along with a huge mirror on the wall.

My hostel mates were very good and it did not take much time for me to cop up with them as I had Dimple one of my classmates as well as my hostel mate. So I had a company for the whole day. The orientations and other programmers were completed in the initial few days of our college starting. I was a little afraid and would sometimes cry at night getting scared of this new world but I knew I had to live in it.

Soon I also became good friends with some of my classmates. Trishna Dave-Rutu, a typical Gujarati girl from nearby place Rajpipla. She is my best friend and I love to spent time with her as she is alike me a little afraid of facing the world and new people. She is my secret-knower and the best part of us being alone is clicking endless selfies. I love to be with her because even after several small-big fights between us I know she will stay beside me forever to handle my carless things. Dimple and Ruti knew each other as they both belonged to Rajpipla.

Another guy was Ankush Tripathi, who belonged to Silvassa. I had not heard about the place before I met him. He was a cool and friendly when I first met him. He usually had a good cop up to talk with girls in his first attempt. He was like my brother and was also a very helpful person.

He had an elder brother Shivansh who also belonged to Silvassa. Though there were fights between me and Shivansh on small topics but still we had our friendship bond which would be always important to me.

Yuvi-Saanu was another guy who belonged to Karjan. He was a boy who believed to chase in his dreams, who had a good explaining power and also who was one of my best friend once. We used to fight on small topics but it just added some strength to our friendship which was ruined after a small misunderstanding between us.

Divya Patel, who was from Mumbai. She was a free-minded girl who could take a stand of her own. She had a good debating power which helped her to win over any controversy. She was kind hearted by nature and also a good friend of mine.

Vinay Patel, who belonged to Ankleshwar. He was the person whom I liked the most as he was never upset and always had a smile on his face. He usually cracked funny jokes which make everyone laugh and make a pleasant mood in the group.

Ritu Patel, a localite from Baroda who was a dearer friend of mine, who helped to live alone when no one stayed by my side and who always supported me in every manner. She was whole-hearted and lived life to the fullest.

Apart from them I had Parth, Kenil, Deepika and most of my class mates. They all were my classmates as well. The people with whom I spent almost half a day every day. The people whom I had a different experience.

Prateik Joshi, the most important person in my life and my bestest friend-my Dhondu-my face book friend and who is the one I would never wish to loose-the one who is the there for me whenever I need him. Though he was away from me and studied in different institute, we lived in the same city, and even after innumerable fights he was the one who always remembered me that he was by my side whenever I needed him. No one will ever replace his place no matter innumerable people come and go.

Utkarsh Chandnani, an automobile engineer and also a surti also my guide. He was one of the closest friend in my group who was ready to listen to all my crazy stuffs whenever I used to call him and he also was the one who would advice me to every problem in my life.

Neel Patel, another surti and an automobile engineer who was also the guide to me. "Poplu" as he usually called me was one of the friends who listened to me when I was silent. He could easily get to know anything about my mood. Though he was the silent person of our group, he was the most mischievous friend who loved to play different pranks at his hostel. Whenever we met there was no day when we would do something silly which added to the memory list.

Harsh Trivedi, a Mumbaikar was one of the cutest friend of mine who was never indulged to get serious. He always had a jolly mood playing different thoughts and pranks in his mind. He was cool and friendly-supportive and joyous.

Kishan Ahi, Dha-val and Hardi Patel were my friends from Rajkot. Bhumi and Devu are my hostel mates.

These were the people who were with me after the life which I left behind in Surat. We are the people who would end up biding goodbyes to each other after four years when we would depart from each other with innumerable memories.

It has been a year with these people now. Many ups and downs were seen by me as Life does not move smoothly.

"Too much of anything creates an imbalance in life"

Fights, birthday memories, late night dinners, movie planning's, drives and innumerable memories are the things I got from these people. No matter nobody is going to stay by each other's side but friendship is something which stays till the end.

I'm glad to share the most precious moments of my life with these gems of my life. Whether it is a Navratri celebration or a Diwali or Holi. Every festival reminds me of a memory we created till now.

Birthdays just remember of the cake we cut behind our canteen area and spoil the cake applying on each other's face and eating almost every item from the food court on every birthday.

Traditional days or Superhero days or Signature days-every day has a different meaning and different fun. Though we would never stay by each other's side after a little span of time but they will remain as a forever picture.

A year has passed like in a blink of the eye with these people today here because they teach me to love, to live, to play, to smile, to laugh, to learn, to fight and atlast to forget someone whom I thought I never would. I am happy without Rehan today on the tenth of June.

"I'M HAPPY WITHOUT THE PERSON I ONCE THOUGHT I NEEDED THE MOST"

He is always in my mind and my heart even today as the person whom I loved the most. But I have learned to live without him. As time heals everything as we gradually proceed in life. There is someone waiting for me to fill his place into my life-who loves me the same way I loved him. Who will make me smile the way I smiled looking at him and for whom I'll be his everything. ☺

The woods are lovely, dark and deep,

But I have promises to keep,

And miles to go,

Before I sleep!

"If all perished and he remained, I should continue to be;
And if all else remained and he were annihilated,
The universe would turn to be a mighty stranger!"
"In that word, beautiful in all languages,

But most in yours, Amor mio is compromised my existence here and hereafter,

I feel I exist here, and

I feel exist hereafter- to what purpose you will decide, my destiny rests with you.

But I more than love you,

And cannot cease to love you.

Think of me, sometimes when the Alps and oceans divide us-but they never unless you wish it.

I wake filled with thoughts of you. Your portrait and the intoxicating evening when I used to see you secretly have left my senses in turmoil.

Sweet, incomparable me,

What a strange effect he has on my heart!

Yielding to the profound feelings,

Which overwhelm me, until then a thousand seeing but give me none in return?

For they set my blood in fire."

When I was sure of losing, I won...

When I needed people the most, they left me...

When I learned to dry out tears, I got a shoulder to cry...

When I became busy, I got friends...

When I mastered the skill to hate, somebody started loving me...

When, after waiting for my love, dawn emerged...

I fell asleep when the sun came out...

So I prayed to God to rewind my life cycle.

Baby, you have risen up my world like no one else did.

--The way he nodded his head even if he did not understand anything.

--The way he moved his legs here and there.

--The way he used to come last minute to the class. "OHH!! HOW CAN I FORGET??" The day I first saw him was the day too he came late.

--The day when she comes to know his name when he gave her the assignment pushing his hand through it slightly.

--The day when she first heard his voice spelling "CEAT-TYRES".

--The day when she came to know that he was accompanying her in board exams.

--The day when he suddenly stood in front of her and she was panic-stricken which gave her butterflies in her stomach.

--The day he gave her pencil and she gave him his and he replied by saying a "THANK-YOU" in the sweetest tone.

--The days when she did not got a glimpse to see him...

--The days before her birthday when it was her first birthday with him and she was excited a month ago.

--The days she used to sit in tests besides him on the same bench.

--*The day when he said "NO" I don't like her!!!!*

--*The days when our classes together ended....*

--*The day when she came to know that it was his birthday that evening.*

--*The days she used to call him from unknown numbers and harass him to listen to his voice.*

--*The separation days when she used to search for him after each and every class.*

--*The days he used to stare at her without a single blink of the eye.*

--*The days he used to wear the clothes color she wore the previous day.*

--*The way he played with his hairs almost making it messy all the time.*

--*The day when she saw him for the last time.*

--*The day when she talked with him for the first time in her life!*

--*The day when he called her and talked on the phone for 1 hour.*

--*The day he told her he doesn't like her and likes her sister.*

--*The day they met and for the last time.*

--*The days she cried...*

--*The days she laughed...*

--The days she smiled…

--The days she never wanted to lose…

--The days she never wanted to forget….

--The days she missed him the most…

--The days she needed him the most…

--The days she loved him the most…

--THE DAYS WERE GONE!!!

"AND SHE WAS HAPPY WITHOUT THE PERSON SHE THOUGHT SHE ONCE NEEDED THE MOST!"

"BECAUSE SHE LOVED A PERSON WHO NEVER LOVED HER!"

AND WHAT WASHES AWAY IN THE TEARS, IS NEVER BROUGHT BACK THROUGH A SMILE……" ☺☺☺☺☺